The Only Way Out is In

Written by Alanna Zabel
Illustrated by Rita Vigovszky

Published by AZIAM Books
© 2001 Alanna Zabel
All Rights Reserved
ISBN: 978-0989807760

www.aziam.com

AZIAM
BOOKS

Dedicated to:

The Next Generation of Yogi's

She sat in the center of the labyrinth.
Waiting, waiting, waiting.
It was her liberation
That she was greatly anticipating.

She was Sama, the dark Goddess,
Prophecized to return.
To heal the world with love,
Praying that people would learn.

She was hidden behind a wall.
Which only she could see straight through.
Others could not see inside,
Unless their love was pure and true.

Many great warriors
Have embarked on the challenging quest
Of unveiling this powerful goddess
If they could successfully pass her tests.

There were three tests to pass:
1) Physical, 2) Mental, and 3) Emotional.
Many passed the Physical test,
But none have passed them all.

What truly impressed the Goddess
Was his humble gratitude.
He knelt to give thanks,
He didn't strike an arrogant attitude.

The next test to pass
Involved a Mental riddle.
He was given measurements to calculate
The fastest route to the labyrinth's middle.

Intelligent and precise,
The warrior found the center fast.
He nimbly ran the course,
Facing her wall at last.

The Goddess was very excited.
She was praying on her knees.
She would be free at last,
If he trusts what he believes.

To pass the final test,
He must act on how he feels.
Then the powerful Goddess
Would finally be revealed.

A spider crawled along the wall.
He whispered, "This is your test."
"You must choose one of two women,"
"Whom you believe is the true goddess."

Two women appeared in front of him.
One was very physically attractive.
She dressed in tight, seductive clothing.
"Aren't I beautiful?" she asked him.

Her sight was an oasis.
From the warrior's journey alone.
He asked what her name was.
She replied, "Errone."

The other woman next to her
Was simply dressed and appeared more shy.
Yet there was a sweetness about her,
That radiated strongly from her eyes.

"But she can't be a Goddess," he thought,
"Beauty is a gift of the Divine."
"But Errone is rather arrogant,"
"I can't make up my mind!"

"You have to choose me!" Errone insisted,
Placing her hands on her hips.
The other woman said nothing.
She formed a smile upon her lips.

Deeply moved by her sweet smile,
The warrior momentarily lost his voice.
After a few moments he cleared his throat,
Announcing, "Errone is my choice!"

The Goddess exhaled all of her breath.
Then she fell to the ground.
Discouraged that the warrior
Had failed the final round.

"Now what do I do?"
The trapped Goddess cried.
The spider crawled under her wall, whispering,
"There's something you haven't tried."

"You can set yourself free," he said.
"For a hero you need not wait."
"I will teach you the 8 Limbs of Yoga,"
"That will liberate your fate."

The spider's name was Ashta.
In Sanskrit "Ashta" means "Eight."
Ashtanga is the 8-Limbed Path
That Patanjali did create.

Living by these standards
You will receive countless graces.
Any falseness will disappear
As will any negativity or hatred.

Ashta held up one of his legs.
"Yama is the first limb."
"Try not to lie, steal or hurt anyone,"
"Choose not to sin."

"When you control your senses,"
"You will develop Self-mastery."
"Don't be ruled by your desires,"
"Which will only lead to misery."

1: YAMA

"Niyama is the second limb."
"Devotion to God through your work."
"Keep your body clean and modest."
"It is the vessel through which you serve."

The Goddess Sama then repeated,
"Be honest, clean, and true,"
"Know myself and serve God,"
"Through all that I do."

2: NIYAMA

"Speaking of the body," Ashta said,
"Asana is Ashtanga's third limb."
"These physical postures of Yoga,"
"Keep your energy channels open."

"To guide this energy through your body,"
"Learn to control your life force."
"Practice Pranayama, or breath control."
"This is yoga limb number four."

Sama sat on the ground,
Crossing her legs into Lotus Pose.
She lifted her back straight,
Watching the breath flow through her nose.

4: PRANAYAMA

"You are doing great!" said Ashta,
"And you're halfway through."
"Pratyahara is the fifth limb,"
"Detaching from everything. Even you."

5: PRATYAHARA

"By withdrawing from your senses,"
"You surrender any attachments and goals."
"Observing instead of seeking,"
"Accept and trust this natural flow."

"Continue with your practice," Ashta said.
"The next phase will arise naturally."
"You will feel deep love and union"
"With all living beings, you will see."

7: DHYANA

"This is Dhyana."
"The seventh leg of this wheel."
"Samadhi is the eighth and final limb."
"Where only the present moment is real."

Slowly and quietly Ashta crawled away
As Sama was in a deep state of bliss.
In her many years of seeking freedom,
It was only herself that she had missed.

A light began to radiate
From the center of her heart.
It became so intense,
That it broke her wall apart!

Using Yoga to reveal her true self,
Sama worked from the inside out
You, too, can follow these guidelines.
And you will succeed, I have no doubt.

Patanjali's 8 Limbs of Yoga

1. Yama
self *restraint*

2. Niyama
observances

3. Asana
posture & movement

4. Pranayama
breath control

5. Pratyahara
withdrawal of senses

6. Dharana
intense focus, steady mind

7. Dhyana
contemplation, meditation

8. Samadhi
oneness, bliss

Made in the USA
San Bernardino, CA
18 May 2018